OLIVER'S TALES - SEEKING WISDOM

Copyright © 2023 by Spirit & Truth

All rights reserved.

Printed in the United States of America. No part of this book may be used or reproduced in any manner whatsoever without written permission except in the case of brief quotations embodied in critical articles or reviews.

For information contact:
SPIRIT & TRUTH
PO BOX 1737
MARTINSVILLE, IN 46151

spiritandtruthonline.org

Written by Kelli Young
Illustrations and Cover design by Hanif Roihan
ISBN: 9781088172711

First Edition: September 2023

10 9 8 7 6 5 4 3 2 1

OLIVER'S TALES: SEEKING WISDOM

Proverbs 3:13-16
"Blessed is the person who finds Wisdom, and the one who obtains discernment, for the gain from her is better than the gain from silver, and her revenue is better than gold. She is more precious than gems, and no delightful thing can compare to her. "

It was a gloomy gray day in God's Country. It had been raining outside all day. Annie and her Great Dane, Oliver, had been playing outside for a while, splashing in puddles and getting soaked through and through. Annie's younger brother Jacob had joined in until his boots got full of water, and he retreated inside for dry socks and a snack.

After a while, Annie and Oliver went inside to dry off and find a comfortable spot on the couch to read.

"I do like playing in the rain, but I'm glad I didn't live during the time of Noah; forty days and forty nights of rain seems like too much to me!" Oliver said as he curled up on his dog bed.

"Yeah, that doesn't seem like much fun to me either. Oliver, how do you know so much about God and the Bible?" asked Annie.

"I've been very blessed to have some great mentors in my life who have taught me how to seek God. Your mom and dad have taught me a lot. They really love God, and you all are always reading the Bible and memorizing new verses," said Oliver. He got a big smile on his face and a twinkle in his eye when he started to talk again. "But if you want to know how I first came to know God, I'll have to tell you about when I was a pup."

"Oh, wow! I don't think you've ever told me about when you were little before," said Annie excitedly.

"You see, Annie, not every person, or every pup, is born into a wonderful home like this one. I was born in a very different place and I'm so glad that I found my way to you and your family," said Oliver.

"Oh, what kind of place were you born in?" Annie asked.

"In a place called Alabama, in the wilderness of a busy city," Oliver answered.

I don't remember too much about the very beginning, but I do remember being very lonely. I never found out what happened to my mom and dad, but it was me and my pup brothers and sisters all by ourselves. We were all very sick and very little, and we didn't have any food or water. When we had all just about given up hope that anyone would come and find us, that's when Lynnie rescued us."

"She came into that darkness where we all were and carried us out one by one. She brought us to a home that was warm and full of light. There were warm blankets and fresh water, and best of all, food. There were others there too, helping with things, but mostly I remember Lynnie. She was so big, all ten of us pups could curl up by her belly and sleep for the night."

"As we were all trying to recover, Lynnie would sing to us. I didn't know it then, but she was singing David's Psalms. She sang one often; I still remember it...

Yahweh is my shepherd, I will not lack.
He makes me lie down in green pastures.
He leads me beside still waters.
He restores my soul.
He guides me in the paths of righteousness for his name's sake.
Even though I walk through the valley of the shadow of death,
I will fear no evil, for you are with me.
Your rod and your staff, they comfort me.

You prepare a table before me in the presence of my enemies.
You anoint my head with oil. My cup runs over.
Surely goodness and covenant faithfulness will pursue me all the days of my life, and I will dwell in Yahweh's house for my length of days.
(Psalm 23)

"Each day, all my brothers and sisters got stronger. I was the runt, the smallest of us, so I wasn't bouncing back like everyone else was. I didn't seem to be getting much better. A lot of the other dogs around didn't think I could make it. I was just too small. But Lynnie wasn't going to give up on me, so she went out on a long trek to get the medicine I needed from some humans she had befriended."

"When she got back, everyone told her it was too late. It had taken too long. There was no way the medicine would help now. But Lynnie was determined.

She said, 'God told me to save these pups. He told me where they were and that all ten would live. I know God has a plan for this pup. He may be small, but he is strong.' I didn't know who God was, but I knew that He must be someone good if He was a friend of Lynnie's."

"Then Lynnie and all the dogs there circled around me and prayed. They asked God to heal me and give me strength. I had never heard anything like it, but I knew that it was powerful. She gave me some of the medicine she brought back, and then I slept. But it wasn't like the sleep I had before. Before, I was restless and achy, and it was cold. Now I slept peacefully, and I could feel myself getting stronger even though I wasn't awake."

"A few days later, I woke up. I knew in my bones I was going to be fine. I felt stronger than I ever had before. I stood up and gave a 'yip', and everyone turned to look at who had made that noise. Everyone came bounding over. My brothers and sisters were jumping and licking and barking. No one could believe how good I looked."

"Lynnie padded over and said in her gentle yet strong voice, 'Oliver, God has saved your life from the clutches of evil. You are a miracle. The only thing that can stop you now is foolishness.'

From that moment on, I wanted to know everything I could about this God. I followed Lynnie everywhere and asked her question after question about who He was and why He saved me."

"Lynnie taught me all that she could in the short time that we had together. She told me stories from the Bible, she told me about God's love for me, but most importantly she taught me about Jesus. She taught me how Jesus was God's Son and how he lived and sacrificed his life for us.

How he died on a cross and then God raised him from the dead. And that if I believed in Jesus and his resurrection, then I could live forever; that I didn't have to be afraid of sickness or death anymore.

And eventually we would live on a new earth where there wouldn't be any of these horrible things ever again."

"I wanted to stay with Lynnie and all the dogs there forever, but Lynnie said that wasn't possible. She said this was her path, and we all needed to find ours. One by one, all of my brothers and sisters got taken by rescuers to live with families in nice homes. I was the last of us. Every time someone would come to take a pup, I would always run and hide. I wasn't ready to leave.

There were more pups that came in every day, it seemed. Lynnie was always rescuing pups off the streets. That was her duty, she said. She had been doing it for so long, and she said she would keep doing it until every pup was saved or God told her to stop."

"Finally my day came. There were only a handful of us left on the truck. We stopped, and the humans opened the door and the most beautiful smells came in through the door. They came right for my kennel and said, 'It's your turn, Oliver.'

I was so excited I could hardly let myself be carried out. I remember hearing you and Jacob squeal and giggle as soon as he carried me out the door. He put me down and you both surrounded me and I was so excited. You got on your knees and whispered in my ear, "God told me about you in my dream, Oliver. We're going to take care of you now."

"Yeah, I remember that day. You were so tiny. At first I was a little surprised, because in my dream you were this big dog, and when you came out of the truck you were so small. But I knew it was you," Annie chimed in.

I'm so glad to be here with you and your family. I often think about Lynnie. I know she's doing exactly what God wants her to do, and I think I am, too. I always try to seek God and His wisdom in every situation, so I don't get led astray by foolishness."

"Is that why you're always quoting Proverbs?" asked Annie.

"Absolutely," said Oliver. "That was Lynnie's warning to me after I got healed. I don't want to become a fool, but instead I want to seek after wisdom."

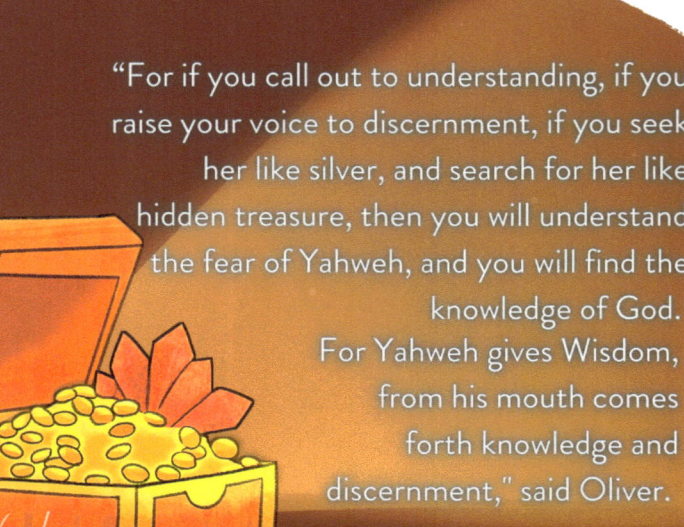

"For if you call out to understanding, if you raise your voice to discernment, if you seek her like silver, and search for her like hidden treasure, then you will understand the fear of Yahweh, and you will find the knowledge of God. For Yahweh gives Wisdom, from his mouth comes forth knowledge and discernment," said Oliver.

(Proverbs 2:3-6)

"Lynnie was a great mentor to me. She taught me so much about God and the Bible. I'm thankful that she chose to use wisdom and save so many of us."

Printed in the USA
CPSIA information can be obtained
at www.ICGtesting.com
LVHW070305090923
756292LV00011B/61